OKLAHOMA

Julie Murray

VISIT US AT
www.abdopublishing.com

Published by ABDO Publishing Company, PO Box 398166, Minneapolis, MN 55439.

Printed in the United States of America, North Mankato, Minnesota.
052012
092012

PRINTED ON RECYCLED PAPER

Coordinating Series Editor: Rochelle Baltzer
Editor: Sarah Tieck
Contributing Editors: Megan M. Gunderson, BreAnn Rumsch, Marcia Zappa
Graphic Design: Adam Craven
Cover Photograph: *iStockphoto*: ©iStockphoto.com/flashpoint.
Interior Photographs/Illustrations: *Alamy*: Brady Mays (p. 29); *AP Photo*: AP Photo (pp. 23, 25, 27), Cal Sport Media via AP Images (p. 26), Muskogee Daily Phoenix, Jerry Willis (p. 26); *Getty Images*: Samuel D. Barricklow (p. 19), Annie Griffiths/National Geographic (p. 27), HITOSHI KAWAKAMI/amanaimagesRF (p. 30), MPI (p. 13); *iStockphoto*: ©iStockphoto.com/chrisp0 (p. 9), ©iStockphoto.com/Davel5957 (p. 11), ©iStockphoto.com/jcrader (p. 30), ©iStockphoto.com/sharply_done (p. 21), ©iStockphoto.com/JustinVoight (p. 5); *Shutterstock*: Marie C Fields (p. 30), Philip Lange (p. 30), val lawless (p. 9), Josh Resnick (p. 27), Guy J. Sagi (p. 17), Victorian Traditions (p. 13).

All population figures taken from the 2010 US census.

Library of Congress Cataloging-in-Publication Data

Murray, Julie, 1969-
 Oklahoma / Julie Murray.
     p. cm. -- (Explore the United States)
  ISBN 978-1-61783-374-8
 1. Oklahoma--Juvenile literature. I. Title.
 F694.3.M87 2013
 976.6--dc23
                              2012015706

OKLAHOMA

Contents

ONE NATION

The United States is a **diverse** country. It has farmland, cities, coasts, and mountains. Its people come from many different backgrounds. And, its history covers more than 200 years.

Today the country includes 50 states. Oklahoma is one of these states. Let's learn more about Oklahoma and its story!

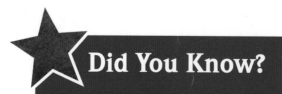

Did You Know?

Oklahoma became a state on November 16, 1907. It was the forty-sixth state to join the nation.

OKLAHOMA UP CLOSE

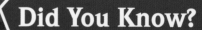
The United States has four main **regions**. Oklahoma is in the South.

Oklahoma has six states on its borders. Colorado and Kansas are north. Missouri and Arkansas are east. Texas is south and west. New Mexico lies to the west.

Oklahoma has a total area of 69,899 square miles (181,038 sq km). About 3.8 million people live there.

REGIONS OF THE UNITED STATES

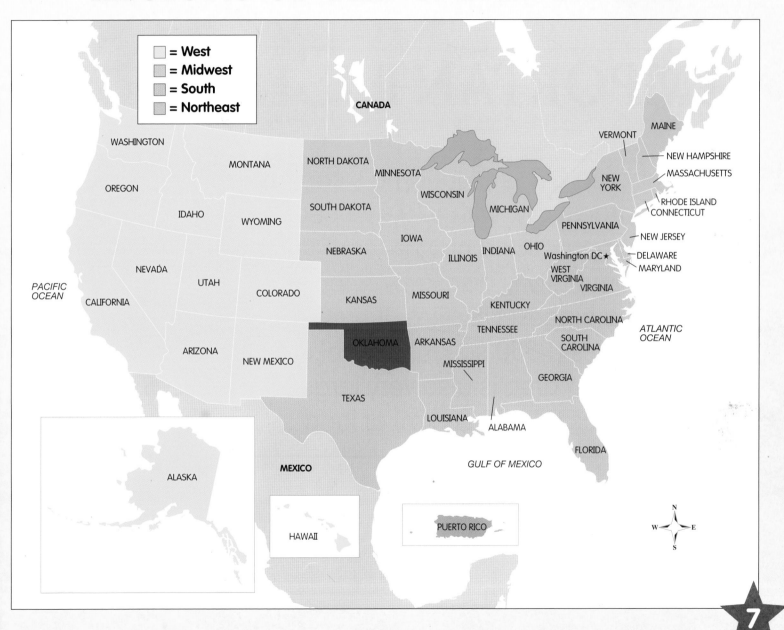

= West
= Midwest
= South
= Northeast

CANADA

WASHINGTON
MONTANA
NORTH DAKOTA
MINNESOTA
VERMONT
MAINE
NEW HAMPSHIRE
MASSACHUSETTS
OREGON
IDAHO
WYOMING
SOUTH DAKOTA
WISCONSIN
MICHIGAN
NEW YORK
RHODE ISLAND
CONNECTICUT
PENNSYLVANIA
NEW JERSEY
NEVADA
UTAH
COLORADO
NEBRASKA
IOWA
ILLINOIS
INDIANA
OHIO
Washington DC ★
WEST VIRGINIA
DELAWARE
MARYLAND
PACIFIC OCEAN
CALIFORNIA
ARIZONA
NEW MEXICO
KANSAS
MISSOURI
KENTUCKY
VIRGINIA
TENNESSEE
NORTH CAROLINA
SOUTH CAROLINA
ATLANTIC OCEAN
OKLAHOMA
ARKANSAS
MISSISSIPPI
GEORGIA
TEXAS
LOUISIANA
ALABAMA
FLORIDA
GULF OF MEXICO
MEXICO
ALASKA
HAWAII
PUERTO RICO

N
W E
S

7

IMPORTANT CITIES

Oklahoma City is Oklahoma's **capital**. It is also the state's largest city, with 579,999 people. The city is known for producing oil.

Oklahoma City is also known for its size. It is one of the biggest US cities. It has more than 600 square miles (1,550 sq km) of total area! The city's **metropolitan** area is also very large. It covers 5,518 square miles (14,292 sq km) of land.

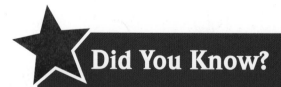

Did You Know?

Oklahoma City became the capital in 1910. Guthrie was the capital before that.

Oklahoma

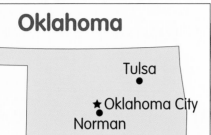

Tulsa

★ Oklahoma City

Norman

N W E S

The Oklahoma State Capitol is in one of the area's major oil fields. There is an oil well on the grounds, but it stopped producing oil in 1986.

Oklahoma City is home to many large businesses. Sonic Drive-In restaurants are based there.

Tulsa is Oklahoma's second-largest city, with 391,906 people. The Arkansas River splits the city into two parts. Tulsa is known for producing oil.

Norman is the state's third-largest city. It is home to 110,925 people. This historic city was built around a Santa Fe Railroad **depot**.

Tulsa has many green plants and trees. It looks different from much of Oklahoma, which is drier.

OKLAHOMA IN HISTORY

Oklahoma's history includes Native Americans and settlers. For thousands of years, Native American tribes lived on the land. They hunted, fished, farmed, and gathered wild food.

Beginning in 1830, Native Americans from around the country were forced to move to the Indian Territory. Present-day Oklahoma was part of this land. In 1889, some of the land was given to white settlers. In 1907, Oklahoma became a state.

12

In 1889, new settlers lined up and raced to claim land in Oklahoma. This was called a land run.

Did You Know?

Some of the new settlers moved to the land before they were supposed to. They were called "sooners." That is why Oklahoma is called "the Sooner State."

After the 1889 land run, Oklahoma's population grew quickly. Settlers lived in tents while they built new cities.

Timeline

1803

President Thomas Jefferson bought land for the United States as part of the **Louisiana Purchase**. The land included present-day Oklahoma.

1889

Settlers claimed land in Oklahoma in a famous land run.

1907

Oklahoma became the forty-sixth state on November 16.

1800s

Cherokee Native Americans from the southern states were forced to move to the Indian Territory. They faced hunger, sickness, and cold. Thousands died. The move became known as "the Trail of Tears."

The first large oil well was drilled in Bartlesville.

1897

1838

1928

Oil was discovered in Oklahoma City. At its peak, the city had about 1,400 producing wells.

2011

A set of tornadoes touched down in May. People died and buildings were torn apart throughout the state. One of the tornadoes struck an area 50 miles (80 km) long!

1900s

2000s

Oklahoma City became the state **capital**.

1910

A **bomb** destroyed the Alfred P. Murrah Federal Building in Oklahoma City. It killed 168 people.

1995

15

ACROSS THE LAND

Oklahoma has mountains, **plains**, lakes, rivers, and forests. The Sandstone Hills, Ouachita (WAH-shuh-taw) Mountains, and Wichita Mountains are in the state. Major rivers include the Red and the Arkansas Rivers.

Many types of animals make their homes in Oklahoma. These include horned toads, water moccasin snakes, and bison.

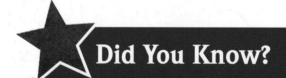

Did You Know?

In July, the average temperature in Oklahoma is 82°F (28°C). In January, it is 37°F (3°C).

Some parts of Oklahoma are grassy and green. Others are dry and have cactus plants.

Tornado Alley

Oklahoma is located in Tornado Alley. This part of the United States is known for having many tornadoes.

A tornado is a spinning, twisting funnel of air. Most tornadoes last for just a few minutes. But they can last more than an hour.

Tornadoes are very powerful and can tear apart towns. Some have winds as fast as 300 miles (480 km) per hour!

Did You Know?

Tornado Alley also includes Kansas, Texas, and Nebraska.

Tornadoes are common in the flat, grassy lands of Oklahoma from April to June.

19

EARNING A LIVING

Oklahoma has important businesses. Many people have jobs with the government or helping visitors to the state. Some work at US Air Force bases. Others work for companies that make food or machinery.

Oklahoma has many natural **resources**. Cattle **ranches** and oil fields are found on its land. Farms provide wheat, dairy products, cotton, and soybeans.

Oil is one of Oklahoma's most important products. At oil wells, it is removed from the ground.

Hometown Heroes

Many famous people are from Oklahoma. Baseball player Mickey Mantle was born in Spavinaw in 1931.

From 1951 to 1968, Mantle played for the New York Yankees. He was a great home run hitter. He hit 536 home runs during his career! In 1974, he joined the National Baseball Hall of Fame.

Will Rogers was born in Oologah in 1879. At that time, Oklahoma was part of the Indian Territory.

Rogers started out as a cowboy. Later, he appeared in Wild West shows. Over time, he became a famous entertainer.

Rogers was known for his sense of humor. He gave speeches and wrote for newspapers. Rogers was also in movies and on the radio. And, he wrote six books!

Rogers often dressed like a cowboy. He loved showing his cowboy skills, such as using a lasso.

25

Tour Book

Do you want to go to Oklahoma? If you visit the state, here are some places to go and things to do!

 **See**

Learn about Native Americans at Cherokee Heritage Center near Tahlequah. The center puts on plays and has an ancient village display.

 Cheer

Watch a University of Oklahoma football game! Over the years, the Sooners have won seven national championships!

Remember

Learn about Route 66, a famous American highway that crosses Oklahoma. There are two Route 66 museums in the state. One is in Clinton and the other is in Elk City.

Listen

Take in some live music at Cain's Ballroom in Tulsa. It was built in 1924 and became known for western swing music.

Eat

Have a steak or a hamburger and drink some milk. Oklahoma is known for its cattle ranches and dairy farms.

27

A GREAT STATE

The story of Oklahoma is important to the United States. The people and places that make up this state offer something special to the country. Together with all the states, Oklahoma helps make the United States great.

Route 66 passes through Oklahoma. This famous road is also called the Will Rogers Highway.

Fast Facts

Date of Statehood:
November 16, 1907

Population (rank):
3,751,351
(28th most-populated state)

Total Area (rank):
69,899 square miles
(19th largest state)

Motto:
"Labor Omnia Vincit"
(Labor Conquers All Things)

Nickname:
Sooner State

State Capital:
Oklahoma City

Flag:

Flower: Oklahoma Rose

Postal Abbreviation:
OK

Tree: Eastern Redbud

Bird: Scissor-Tailed Flycatcher

Important Words

bomb (BAHM) a weapon made to explode when set off.
capital a city where government leaders meet.
depot (DEE-poh) a railroad station.
diverse made up of things that are different from each other.
Louisiana Purchase land the United States purchased from France in 1803. It extended from the Mississippi River to the Rocky Mountains and from Canada through the Gulf of Mexico.
metropolitan of or relating to a large city, usually with nearby smaller cities called suburbs.
plains flat or rolling land without trees.
ranch a large farm where people raise cattle, horses, or sheep.
region a large part of a country that is different from other parts.
resource a supply of something useful or valued.

Web Sites

To learn more about Oklahoma, visit ABDO Publishing Company online. Web sites about Oklahoma are featured on our Book Links page. These links are routinely monitored and updated to provide the most current information available.

www.abdopublishing.com

Index

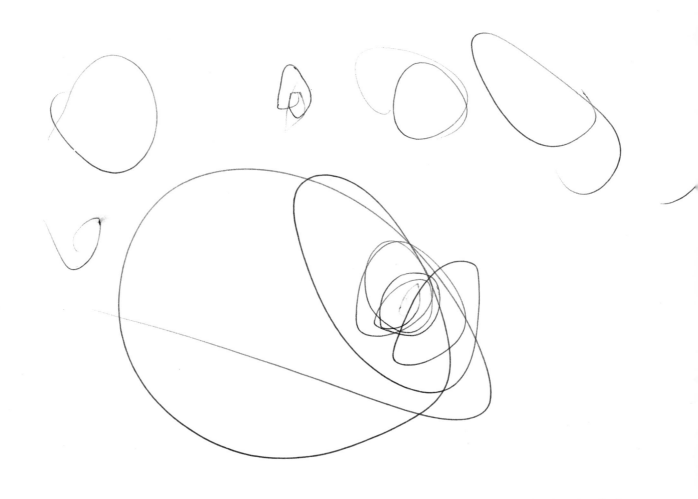